CALBERT: The Third-Grade Cowboy

Facing the Bully

Lisa Head

For my Wonderful Boys

Aiden, Randy and Jesse

TABLE OF CONTENTS

Calbert: The Third-Grade Cowboy Facing the Bully

Chapter 1
A Cowboys Work is Never Done

"Bang bang bang!" Calbert shouted. He pulled his six-shooters out of his holster and darted around the corner to his big brother's bedroom. "Take that!" He said, pointing his pistol at imaginary bad guys. Jason yelled at him, "Get lost, kid!"

"Kid! Who are you calling a kid? I am Calbert, the toughest cowboy in the third grade," Calbert yelled back. "Even my name means 'cowboy,' so there."

He moved into the kitchen. *You never know what kind of outlaw may have stopped for a bite. Especially if they had fresh baked chocolate chip cookies on their minds.* "Bang bang bang!" He shot again, only to find his little brother staring back at him. *He's the real "kid" around here.* Ethan is Calbert's baby brother. *Ethan is very annoying.*

Ethan looked at him and said, "Calbert, Calbert, Calbert, will you play with me?"

"If you'll play cowboys," Calbert answered.

"No way," Ethan replied and then hopped out of the kitchen.

I sure don't know what Mom was thinking when she adopted Ethan along with Jason and me. We have always been brothers, but this was our chance to get rid of him—wish we could give him back! Actually, I do kind of like him, but I'm not going tell him that!

Calbert headed outside, he yelled "Yay, it's Saturday."

My teacher likes me, and I have lots of friends, but then there is Ernie and he likes to pick on me. On Saturdays, I don't have to worry about Ernie at all, just about having fun.

Calbert kept playing "shoot 'em up" games outside. *My black cowboy hat fits me just perfectly, except for the flat part on top.*

Thanks a lot, Ethan!

Chapter 2
Calbert's World

The sunshine felt warm against his face; it was great to be outside.

We had to write about our home in school yesterday. I wrote, we live in northern Indiana. My family and I live in the country and have cornfields all around our house.

We can even watch the cows across the road from our front porch. We have lots of trees on our land. I know the teacher will love it. I bet she'll give me an A.

Boy, this maple tree is tall. It takes a lot of strength, but I can climb it. I will be on the lookout for any bandits that might come along.

I can also watch my brothers and see if there is anything they do that Mom might want to know about.

My black eye is still hurts from Ernie punching me last week. I told everyone I fell down and bumped it on the sidewalk, but that was a lie. He's always coming after me, just can't figure out what to do about it yet.

I told him, "leave me alone!" Ernie just laughed as he stepped over me to go play on the slide. I'll think of something.

Hey, look there! There are some bad guys coming in from the cornfield. He sank lower in the tree so that the outlaws couldn't see him. He pulled his pistol from its holster, and "bang bang bang," *I got him. He won't be bothering anyone anymore.*

Hey, Jason and Ethan are making a fort. "Wait a minute. I'm coming over to play with you." *Jason loves to build teepees and shelters. He is two years older and knows all about those kinds of things.* "Hey, Jason, do you remember the time we made an oven outside using a rock? I hope we get to do that again. It was so cool!"

"Sure, but next time, we are going to to wash the rock off first. The dirt made the hot dogs too crunchy last time." Jason laughed.

Jason is being too bossy and Ethan keeps tearing down my part of the fort. "I'm not playing with you guys anymore." He told Jason.

"Go ahead 'Shorty'." Jason replied

"My legs may be short, but I can run faster than you," he told Jason. "The new shoes got last weekend make me even faster."

Calbert's two dogs were barking again. *I wonder what they are going after. Maybe they had cornered an animal, or maybe something was going on that I might need to take care of with his six-shooters.*

"Nolan, Star!" He yelled as he started walking toward the dogs.

He was almost to the gate when he saw the very familiar red bike coming toward the house. *It's Ernie.* His stomach started to get that funny feeling he always got whenever Ernie was around. His heart was racing, and his hands were beginning to sweat.

I wonder what he is doing at my house. But I feel brave because Ernie never picks on me when my Mom is around. She's one of the teachers at our school.

Slowly, he began walking up to the gate. In his loudest, toughest voice, he shouted, "Who's there?" The kid didn't answer him. *I can't see Ernie's face very well, but I am pretty sure that is his bike.* The rider on the bike had on a light-blue jacket with the hood up over his head. *I can't remember ever seeing Ernie with a light-blue jacket.*

"What do you want?" He asked in his toughest cowboy voice. "Why did you come to my house?" But this time, he whispered it under his breath so Ernie couldn't hear.

Chapter 3
The Tree House

It's Roland! He began walking faster toward the gate. "I thought you were Ernie," He said as they go over to check out Roland's new red bike.

Roland is in the third grade too, but he isn't in my class. He is in Mrs. Holloway's class. "Come on, Roland. Let's go play," he waves his hand toward the tree house.

He'd told Roland about Ernie but make him promise not to tell anyone else. "Ernie would be very mad at me if I told on him," He reminded Roland. "I decided not to tell my mom or my teacher at school. Because I know Ernie will beat me up if I get him in trouble. Just look at my eye!" With a smile, he added, "I haven't told Jason either, because he can't keep a secret."

"Your secret is safe with me," Roland agreed.

"Now let's have some real fun! Let's go and ride the trails"

They zigzag back and forth, dodging trees in every direction. "Roland, your bike is great at jumping hills. It looks like you're flying through the air!" Finally, they reached the middle of the woods and climbed up to the tree house.

"Pull up the rope ladder, Roland."

The tree house is at the top of the largest maple tree we have. It is huge on the inside, with lots of windows. We are able to see for miles around. Roland and I keep really cool stuff up here, like a compass, pocketknife (one my mom doesn't know about), canteen for water, and other things we might need if we had to live here for a while.

Roland and Calbert had also put some cowboy rifles up in the tree house. "This is a great spot to watch for bad guys," Roland said.

"Always good to be prepared you know," Calbert agreed. "Our tree house is the perfect hideout! No one can find us here!" Calbert tells Roland proudly.

On Sunday, after church, Roland came over to play.

Up in the tree house, Calbert told Roland, "Tomorrow it's back to school and I have to see Ernie."

"Ernie gets on the school bus before me. He is always trying to trip me on my way to my seat. He does that every day, and then he always laughs at me when I stumble and fall."

"I'd love to trip him some time so that he would know how it feels. Sometimes he even threatens me that he'll see me at recess and that I'd better watch out."

"I wish it could be the weekend all the time. I love school, but I don't like Ernie. He takes out all the fun out of school. Maybe Ernie will be absent tomorrow."

"Maybe," replied Roland.

Chapter 4
Monday Morning

"Mom, I don't want to get up. Please, just a few more minutes?" Calbert was still tired. He wished school started later in the day. His mom was running around, trying to get everyone ready for school and Ethan ready for the babysitter.

I'd better get up and get dressed before I get in trouble. "Can I wear my new blue-and-white shirt today?" He asked. *I really like that shirt, and so does my teacher.*

Calbert got to wear his new blue-and-white shirt. "Thanks, Mom! Can I wear my holster and six-shooters to school today?"

His mom told him, "No, they are not allowed at school. They'll just have to hang on your bedpost until you get home."

When he hung up his holsters on the bedpost, he told them. "Wish I could wear you to school, and then I bet Ernie would leave me alone. He likes to pick on me a lot. He is just a big bully."

We learned about bullies at school. I wish someone would do something about this one, but he never seems to get caught.

"Get in the car," his mom told the boys. "You have to catch the school bus at the sitter's because I have to be at work early today."

They made it to the sitter's in time to see the flashing lights of the school bus down the road. Calbert's heart was beating really fast, and his hands are starting to sweat a lot. The bus would be there very soon to pick up Jason and Calbert for school.

Jason looked at Calbert and asked, "What's wrong with you?"

But Jason was using his grouchy voice.

So, Calbert just told him "Nothing." Then quietly he said, "I wonder if Ernie is on the bus this morning?" Jason just shrugged his shoulders and looked back down the road for the bus.

The bus came to a stop in front of the driveway. Its yellow flashing lights turned to red, and they waited for the driver to wave for them to get on to the bus. The driver opened the door, and Jason got on first. Calbert started walking up the stairs. *Where is Ernie? Is he on the bus today?* He looked over at Ernie's assigned seat and there he was! Ernie's seat was four rows behind the driver, and he was always sitting in the aisle seat.

Calbert's seat was six rows behind the driver. He shared a seat with Roland, but Roland's mom had driven him to school that day.

He had to get past Ernie. He could hardly get his feet to move. He just knew Ernie was going to try and trip him.

As he moved closer to Ernie, he could see that Ernie's hair was dirty. Calbert could feel Ernie's eyes burning into him. He looked back at Ernie. *Do I look afraid? I don't think so, but maybe I do look a little scared.*

As Calbert got closer, He could tell that Ernie smelled bad. He wondered why Ernie was so dirty. *Probably because he is too mean to take a bath. I bet he tells his mom NO when she tells him to take a shower.*

Calbert had to walk past Ernie. Out went Ernie's foot and he had a huge grin on his face. *I'll just step over it this time,* but Ernie lifted up his leg and was still able to trip Calbert.

He stumbled forward and Calbert landed face first on the floor of the bus. Then he heard Ernie laugh; *I can't stand the way he laughs.*

The bus pulled into school, and Calbert hoped that he didn't have to pass Ernie again. He was trying to wait for Ernie to get off first, but Ernie just sat there.

Everyone else got off the bus, and Calbert was the only one left, except for Ernie. He was left alone to face him. When he started to pass Ernie. Ernie stood up and blocked Calbert from getting off the bus. He tried to look down at the floor, but he could feel Ernie's eyes staring at him.

Calbert's knees felt funny—like they were going to let him fall. His hands were sweaty, his stomach ached, and his body didn't want to move. Finally, he looked up to see Ernie's face. Ernie told Calbert, "I don't like the way you look, and you better watch out because I'm going to plaster you at recess." Then Ernie backed up and grinned. Calbert got off the bus.

He saw a group of his friends up ahead. He yelled, "Wait up, guys, I'm coming!" He ran up to join them. Ernie would not pick on Calbert when he was with a group.

Calbert felt better talking and joking around with his friends as they went into the building.

His friend Mark told his favorite joke. "I'm thirsty. Well, I'm Friday. Come over Saturday, and we'll have a Sunday." They all laughed. "That joke cracks me up every time."

Most of Calbert's friends are in his classroom, so they all walked to class together. Calbert found his locker and put away his jacket. Mrs. Anderson reminded him that it was his week to take care of the class' pet turtle. "Be sure to feed the turtle and to give him fresh water before taking your seat."

Calbert gave the turtle food and fresh water.

Chapter 5
Trouble at the Playground

It was already time for lunch. Mrs. Anderson announced, "We're having pizza today." *Pizza is okay, but I like the school's cheeseburgers better.* Lunch went by quickly, and then it was time for recess. Roland yelled to Calbert, "Come on!"

"I have to get my jacket before I can to go outside and play," Calbert called back.

"Roland, can you believe we're the first ones out here on the playground? It would be awesome if we were the only ones here." He climbed up to the top of the slide and started pretending to shoot bad guys. *Bang bang bang*, using his finger and thumb as a gun. *Bang bang bang*, again Calbert shot at the three bad guys coming up over the hill. Roland managed to shoot the other two.

"*Kapow kapow,* Calbert we make a great cowboy team." "Roland, you are almost as good as me, but I'm still better."

More kids started coming outside. Mrs. Holloway told them, "You boys have to stop your shooting game."

"The grown-ups get upset with us if we pretend to shoot other kids," Roland whispered to Calbert.

"Let's go over by the building and play ball," Calbert whispered back.

"I really like to hang from the monkey bars because I am pretty sure that will make me taller. But playing ball will be okay for now."

"There're too many kids on the monkey bars now anyway," Roland agreed.

"Roland, you're really good at catching and throwing the football." "Hey! That one is way over my head!" Calbert shouted when he tried to jump up and catch it. "I'll get it." He had to run over to the corner of the building to get the ball.

Calbert bent over to pick up the ball, and there was Ernie, glaring at him when he stood up. Ernie pushed Calbert against the wall and in a low quiet voice said, "This is my area, and you can't be here!" Ernie tore a hole in Calbert's shirt when he grabbed him. Calbert just knew Ernie was going to hit him. "You're in for it now," Ernie told Calbert with the corners of his lips squeezed tight. *Where are all the grown-ups?* Calbert wondered. *I can't see any; we are too far around the corner.*

"Leave me alone!" Calbert sneered back.

He must have been gone too long because Roland came around the corner just in time.

"Hey, Calbert, what's taking so long?" Roland then looked right at Ernie and understood.

Ernie looked back at Roland. "You got a problem, little boy?" Ernie looked at Calbert. "You aren't worth my time." Ernie shoved Calbert off to the side and stomped off, laughing.

"I can't stand Ernie; he's so mean. He had better never show up when I have my six-shooters, or he will meet the cowboy in me!" Calbert boasted to Roland.

The bell rang so they had to go back inside.

Chapter 6
Music Class

We go to music class today. It's time to get lined up. I am so excited to go today because we're practicing for a program. It's going to be tomorrow night and our parents and friends can come.

"We're singing all kinds of songs, and some are even about cowboys," I tell Mrs. Anderson with a huge grin. "My favorites are the ones about cowboys!" Calbert told her. "I get to sing a solo in the song 'Home on the Range.'"

That's going to be so much fun. The program is going to be huge; it has all the third graders are singing in it.

Calbert loved to sing and be a cowboy; now he got to do both and in front of everybody. They practiced standing on the risers' correctly and how to move to their songs. *We haven't practiced with the other classes yet, but I think we will soon.* Our music teacher, Mrs. Baldwin, announced, "Since the program is tomorrow night, we will be having a dress rehearsal tomorrow morning."

"I think it means I have to wear my cowboy clothes to school tomorrow," Calbert told the kid next to him. "That'd be so awesome. I'll ask her later if she wants me to wear them or just bring them to school with me."

Mrs. Baldwin laughed when Calbert asked her about his cowboy clothes. She told him, "It'll be okay for you to leave them at home tomorrow."

Calbert didn't know why she laughed. *Oh well, she does things like that sometimes.*

After music, Mrs. Anderson came to take them back to class for the rest of the afternoon. The school day was almost over, and Calbert was ready to go home and play. "Hey, Roland, I'll see you later," he called to Roland in the hallway and waved.

The afternoon bell rang, and Calbert had to gather up his stuff. On the way out to the bus, he talked with Roland, "Can you come over to my house and play tonight?"

"I have to ask my mom, but I bet I can after dinner."

"I can't wait. See you later."

"Are you going to be on the bus tonight?" Calbert asked.

"No, my mom is coming to get me. We have to go shopping, but I will see you after dinner!" said Roland. Calbert could hardly wait. He loved to play with his buddy Roland.

They would always climb up to the tree house and shoot a few bad guys.

Calbert was late getting to the bus because he had talked to Roland too long. And that meant trouble for Calbert.

Chapter 7
Trouble on the Bus

The bus driver told them they could sit anywhere they wanted on the way home. *Sure hope I find a seat far away from Ernie,* Calbert thought when he got on the bus.

He couldn't believe it; the only seat left was the one next to Ernie. *What terrible luck!* He felt his heart start to beat faster, his stomach and head hurt so badly he could hardly think. Ernie was sitting in the aisle seat, so Calbert had to squeeze in between Ernie and the seat in front of them to sit down.

The whole bus was waiting for Calbert to sit down so they could leave. "Sit down!" they all started yelling at him.

"Move your leg, and I will," Calbert told Ernie, but he just laughed and said, "Make me!"

Finally the bus driver yelled, "Let him sit down!" Calbert moved past Ernie and sat next to the window. *Maybe if I just look out the window, he won't try to talk to me.*

It didn't help to look out the window; Ernie talked anyway.

Then all of a sudden, Ernie started teasing Calbert. "You think you're so special because you are adopted." *I didn't even know he knew that about that.* "Your *real* mom didn't want you because you are ugly and stupid. Your mom now doesn't really want you either, but they made her adopt you."

Calbert got very angry. He just couldn't take it anymore, so he yelled at Ernie. "You're just a big fat liar!"

He tried to tell him that it wasn't true that his birth mom did want him and his brothers. *She did want my brothers and me, but she made bad choices, and so she couldn't keep us. She loves us and is glad we are healthy and happy. She just can't take care of us.*

Mom really wanted my brothers and me very badly. She even told us that God didn't let her have babies because He wanted her to wait on us to get here. But he couldn't get any of his words out. So he just sat there all red-faced and wanted to cry. *Ernie so doesn't know what he's talking about.* But when Calbert started crying, Ernie called him a big baby. *I'm not a baby; I wish he'd just get away from me.*

Now what am I going to do? If I get off the bus crying, my mom is going to ask me why. I don't want to tell her what Ernie said about her. I'm afraid it'll hurt her feelings. She always says we can talk about being adopted and ask questions, but I don't very often, except on Gotcha Day.

Gotcha Day is the day Calbert and his brothers became a part of his forever family. They don't do much, but they always talk about the adoption on that day.

Calbert's mom told Ethan that he "came to her only saying three words and with a diaper full of poop." Ethan thinks that is a funny story. Calbert's very happy where he is and loves his new family. They all love him very much too.

Most of the time, I don't even think about being adopted. This is my real family now! How can I tell her what Ernie said? What if she gets mad and calls Ernie's mom? I wish I could talk to Roland before my mom sees me.

Good thing Jason had baseball practice after school. He wasn't around to run in the house and tell their mom that Calbert was crying. He knows Ernie was wrong. He wished he could've thought of better things to say to him.

Nolan ran up to Calbert and licked his face, so Calbert told Nolan about what happened. He looked at Calbert like he understood. "I kind of feel sorry for biological kids because their parents have to take whoever they got. I am lucky because my mom chose me. She picked me out of other kids."

"My family now is great, and we get to go on trips every summer. Last year, we went through the caves in Arkansas and got to do other awesome stuff." *Hey, I'm not crying anymore, and I feel a lot better.* "I better get in the house and do my homework," Calbert told Nolan and patted him on the head. Nolan raced Calbert to the front door.

Chapter 8
A Friend Indeed

They had macaroni and cheese with hot dogs for dinner. That is Calbert's favorite. *It won't be long until Roland gets here. We're going to have so much fun.*

"Mom, why isn't he here yet? Will you call his mom?"

"Just be patient and let him finish his dinner," she told Calbert. Finally, Roland arrived; *let the fun begin!*

"Let's ride our bikes straight to the tree house, Roland. I have my holster and six-shooters."

"And I have my shotgun, so let's go." The corners of Roland's lips curled up into a big smile.

"We'll be able to watch for the bad guys. It's great having all the windows because we can see in every direction. No one can sneak up on us with a surprise attack, not even my annoying brother, Ethan." Calbert gave Roland a big smile and wink.

"Over there, look, ten, maybe twelve, marauders heading right for the tree house," Calbert whispered to Roland. They took cover behind the wall of the tree house and got their pistols and shotguns ready.

"Take off your hat so they can't see it sticking up from under the window," Roland whispered back to Calbert.

"Bang bang bang. There go three." They ducked down while the bullets whiz over their heads.

"Kapow kapow!" shouted Roland. "Just got two of them!" Like a shot, Calbert popped back up, while Roland was reloading.

"Bang bang bang, down goes three more."

"We only have four more to go, and they sure are hard fighters." *The outlaws keep firing at us, and it's making it hard to get back up to shoot at them.* Roland and Calbert looked at each other, nodded their heads, and jumped up shooting. "Yay, we got 'em!" they cheered together.

"Roland, are you excited about the program?" "Boy, am I!"

"I can't wait to sing my solo. I feel like I'm going to throw up when I think about it. But I am still very excited about singing. I wish we both got to sing the solo. That would be awesome!"

Roland managed to squeeze in, "I know it will be great, but I am a little nervous too."

Chapter 9
Good Talk with a Good Buddy

Cutting Roland off, Calbert added, "At least it is a cowboy song I get to sing. I know all those songs. Can you believe that tomorrow night is the night we get to put on our show? My papa is coming to watch too."

"Roland, let's talk." He wanted to tell Roland about how mean Ernie had been to him on the bus. *Here I go again; my throat is hurting from swallowing so fast and no matter how fast I blink, I can feel the tears slide down my cheeks.* "Sorry about crying, but Ernie said some really mean things to me. Don't tell Jason I was crying, okay?"

"Okay." Roland nodded in agreement.

"Oh, Calbert, I forgot, but I wanted to tell you something I heard about Ernie. I heard my mom telling my dad that Ernie's dad died a couple of years ago, and his step dad doesn't really like him. Ernie looks like his dad, and he has the same name as his dad. It makes his step dad jealous of Ernie's dad. Sometimes he gets really mad at Ernie for no reason."

Sitting quietly, Calbert listened intently to what Roland was saying, and finally, he choked out, "I bet there is a good reason he gets mad at Ernie."

"Roland, don't stick up for him. You know what he did at the playground, and wait until you hear what he said to me on the bus."

My throat hurts from swallowing hard and my eyes blink quickly as more tears fall down my cheeks again, "First, Ernie wouldn't let me sit down, and then after the bus driver made him, he made fun of me for being adopted. He said that neither my birth mom nor my mom wanted me and my brothers."

"I think Ernie is mean too, and I am on your side. But I thought you might want to hear the things I heard about Ernie too. I think he is jealous of you because all of your family loves you. And you have friends. All Ernie has is that dog of his to talk to. I hear him talking to that dog all the time when I ride by his house on the way over here."

"Thanks for telling me, Roland. It does make me feel better, but I'm not sure why."

"My mom said too that Ernie's step dad, Chuck, made him get up really early, like while it was still dark, and rake leaves all by himself on Saturday. She says Chuck yells at Ernie a lot more than he does his brother and sisters. I kind of feel bad for Ernie, but he doesn't have to be so mean to everyone."

"It isn't your fault he gets yelled at. We all get yelled at by our parents, but we don't bully other kids," Roland added as he turned to look for more bad guys to shoot.

Chapter 10
What's Up with Ernie?

Ernie watched Munch start jumping in and out of piles of leaves. He laughs out loud. "At least it's Friday, I hate school. I don't know why they make us go anyway, never learn anything." Munch listened intently with his left ear cocked up slightly. "I had five minutes to get dressed and go to the bus. I had to brush my hair down with my hand because I can't find the comb. I have to wear the clothes I wore all weekend because nothing has been washed for a while." Munch's tail wagged quickly as he continues to hang on every word Ernie said. "I'll miss you today."

Ernie's feet scuffed along the floor of the bus as he moved toward his seat; even though he was studying the floor, he knew he would be sitting alone again. *No one else wants to sit by me, but I don't care. Who needs those dorks anyway?* Ernie plopped down into his seat.

Here comes that kid Calbert. He is such an easy mark. I am going to give him the business. Here he comes. Wait wait. Quickly and purposefully, he slid out his right foot just moments before Calbert reached him. Calbert fell face first to the floor. *It is so funny to watch him fall. It makes him so mad. He never says anything, but I can tell by the look on his face. That's what makes it so much fun to mess with him.*

He taunted Calbert with glaring eyes and low voice, "I don't like the way you look and that I am going to get you at recess." Calbert moved past Ernie, without saying a word. "What's the matter, cat got your tongue?" He continued to laugh.

Chapter 11
Ernie and his Rough Monday Morning

Ernie's head was bobbing up and down. He didn't get much sleep the night before. Every time his head dropped past his chin, he jerked his head back up quickly and looked around the room to see if anyone else saw. He tapped his pencil on his desk and hit the toe of his shoe against the leg of his desk.

Ernie's stomach began to churn and make growling noises. He frowned at the other students when they giggle. Ernie looked at the minute hand, and it seemed to move slower and slower; something had to be wrong with the clock. His stomach began to ache more and more; he could smell the pizza from the cafeteria all the way down to his classroom.

Ernie loves the school's pizza. Especially on days like this, when he's so very hungry. Just a few more minutes and his class would finish with their math lesson and would go to lunch.

His whole class could hear his stomach growling loudly. They laughed even harder at Ernie. *I can't wait to get into that pizza.* He ate his pizza, fruit cup, and green beans and drank his milk quickly. He stuffed the food into his mouth as fast as he could chew it.

Seemed like such a long time since his stomach was full. "All the food tastes so good. That is the one good thing about school—we always get to eat."

Ernie managed to stay out of trouble and got to go out for recess after lunch.

He doesn't like recess too much; it lasts too long, and no one ever wants to play with him. *Hey, I see that Calbert kid. Now I am going to have some fun watching that kid squirm. Might as well have some fun as long as I am out here,* he thought as he smiled to himself. *He's with that Roland kid. Roland doesn't rattle as easy as Calbert, so he isn't as much fun to tease.*

He watched as Calbert headed around the corner of the building, chasing a ball. He took a quick look around and didn't see any of the grown-ups. There was his chance. He grabbed Calbert by the collar, and the collar tore a little bit. He didn't mean to rip the collar, *but it happens.*

He was all in Calbert's face when Roland came around the corner. "Ernie let Calbert go." Roland yelled. *Oh well, next time. That Calbert is one goofy kid!*

Ernie went back to class after recess and thought about how he might be able to go to the music program tomorrow night. He was hoping to go but he knows that he probably won't be able to be in the program.

The cowboy songs and stuff we are doing for the program are awesome, but I know I won't be there, so I'll just act like I don't really care. But I do want to be in the program. I think it will be fun. I'm tired of missing out on all the fun stuff. Maybe if I tell my mom and Chuck that it's for a grade, then they will get me to the program.

Chapter 12
Ernie's Bus Ride Home

On the way home on the bus, Calbert had to sit with Ernie. *Poor kid, it was the only seat on the bus.* Ernie felt the anger bubble up inside him; he wasn't sure what it was he was mad about, but someone had to pay. *I think*

Calbert is going to have a heart attack before he sits down. He can sit with me, but I am going to make it tough on him.

Calbert kept looking out the window and wouldn't talk to Ernie. Ernie became even angrier, and he started giving Calbert grief about being adopted. *He's getting all upset and is crying.* Ernie called him a crybaby, but he didn't feel good about what he said. He couldn't understand why he was letting Calbert's crying bother him. But there is no way he is going to let anyone know that.

When Ernie got home, his mom told him, his sister, his two stepsisters, and his stepbrother to go out and play. Ernie could see his mother had been crying again. His step dad, Chuck, wasn't home. Ernie learned not to ask where Chuck was; he would leave, sometimes for days. Ernie and the other kids never knew when Chuck would leave or if he would be coming back. They all learned a long time ago not to ask.

Ernie wanted to play with the other kids, but they were always tattling on him. "No one ever believes my side of the story, and I end up in big trouble," he tells Munch. "I try playing with my sister, but she just wants to play with dolls and all that girly stuff. She really likes having our stepsisters around." Munch cocks his ear. "They play together a lot.

She played with me before they came along." Then sadly, Ernie told Munch, "I would love to play with my stepbrother. He is way bigger than I am, and I think he is kind of cool.

But he just thinks I'm a little kid and doesn't want me hanging around him."

Munch jumped on his chest, and his tail was wagging. He wanted Ernie to play with him. Ernie found a stick, and they play fetch for a long time.

"I think I will go for a bike ride. I have a red bike that my dad gave me just a couple of months before he died," he told Munch. "He was very sick but still made sure I had a great birthday present. He gave me a beautiful fast red bike with hand brakes. Most kids my age don't have the hand brakes and I love them, mostly because my dad gave me the bike." Munch waged his tail in agreement.

It looks old now and needs some work. Ernie has to pump up the tires every time he wants to ride it. It also has started to rust from the snow and rain. "Chuck won't let me keep it in the garage with the other bikes. He says it's an old bike anyway and not important enough to take up room in the garage. But he always lets his kids put their bikes in there for the winter," he tells Munch, who continues to listen. "I don't think Chuck likes me at all, but my mom needs him, so I don't say anything."

Ernie finally got the tires aired up and started riding. He didn't really have anywhere to go, but he likes to ride and pretended he is taking an exciting trip and never coming back.

Sometimes he pretends his bike is his horse, and he is a cowboy riding off into the sunset. Since he didn't really have anywhere to go, he just made figure eight's on the road.

Munch followed him, and he barked at Ernie while he turned circles in the road.

Ernie thinks *Munch must wonder what I'm doing.* Ernie was very grateful to have Munch. He cried when they told him they might not be able to keep Munch when they moved to their new house, but he had gotten lucky when the landlord said Munch could stay.

"Oh boy," he heard Chuck yelling again. "Looks like he is back and letting us all know about it." Munch just looked at him and wagged his tail.

"He's going to make me go back in the house to clean my room. He's always saying I have the dirtiest room of all the kids. It isn't true, but I don't argue with him."

"I better go in and try to clean my room even better Maybe he won't be so mad at me tonight. I just wish that my mom would stick up for me sometimes, but she doesn't." Munch continued to listen and licked him on the nose when Ernie told him, "I cry a lot when nobody else is around."

Lisa Head

Chapter 13
Program Day

"Calbert," he heard his mom call him. He wakes up slowly to the soft glow of the morning sun and to the sounds of birds singing. It was Tuesday, finally! Calbert was now wide-awake and he caught himself singing as he got dressed. "I bet there will be thousands of people there. I will probably be famous after it is all over, but I will still be nice to people. I will have to practice signing my name for all the autographs I am going to have to sign after the program."

His mom kept telling him that he was talking too loud, *but at least I am not jumping up and down like my insides.* Dressed, teeth brushed, and bed made in record time. With his book bag on his arm, he was out the door. Calbert couldn't wait until the program. "Calbert the Singing Cowboy will be singing a cowboy solo for my family and the School!" He shouted as he raced out the door. It was going to be awesome. He bet everyone was going to be there.

"Our dress rehearsal is this morning, and the program is tonight. What a fun day today is going to be. Between practice and recesses, we get to miss a little bit of math class. I love math, but one day is okay." He told his mom.

Without any funny feelings in his stomach or sweaty hands, he started telling Jason about the music program. Jason just kept saying, "I know, I know." The school bus stopped right in front of Calbert. He and Jason got on the bus. *This is the first time since I got up this morning that I have thought about Ernie. After yesterday, I hope to never see Ernie again.*

Walking as slowly as he could, he started moving toward the bus. Jason yelled, "Hurry up!" He walked up the steps and looked around, but there was no Ernie on the bus this morning. he scanned the bus from seat to seat, but he was nowhere to be found.

"I wonder where Ernie is at."

"What?" replied Jason. "Oh, never mind."

As he plopped down next to Roland on the seat, he loudly said, "Hey, Roland, how's it going? Are you excited about the program today?"

"You better believe I am," Roland replied in a much quieter voice, reminding him to watch his volume.

"Think about how much fun today is going to be." He could feel himself starting to smile.

Then he started thinking about what Roland had said to him about Ernie and his step dad. "Roland, do you know anything else about Ernie?"

"Yep, I'll tell you later." Roland answered.

Chapter 14
Dress Rehearsal

When the school bus pulled up in front of the school, Roland and Calbert hopped off the bus and wasted no time catching up with their friends.

"I think I might explode if I don't calm down soon. I'm having a great start to a great day. In a little while, we'll all go down to the gym for the dress rehearsal. I just don't get why they call it a dress rehearsal when you don't really get dressed up in the costumes. That is just plain weird. Don't you think?" He asked Roland.

Finally, they all headed to the gym and lined up in rows by class. Calbert's teacher kept telling him to be still, but it was so hard for him to sit still.

Roland came in and scooted up next to Calbert and began to whisper, "I heard my mom and dad talking this morning about Ernie. My dad said that he heard Ernie talking to his dog Munch on Saturday. Ernie was telling Munch that his face was really cold, and it hurt when he rubbed his eye. My dad said it looked like his eye was swollen."

"He probably got into a fight with someone and they punched him in the eye," Calbert said with a laugh. "I bet he picked on someone tougher than he is and got hit."

"Looks like all the third graders are here." He told Roland. "Ernie wasn't on the bus. I wonder if he will be here today."

Then Calbert spotted Ernie. "There he is, that awful and mean Ernie," he whispered with a huge sigh. "I wonder why he picks me out to be mean to all the time."

Ernie's class was sitting four rows behind Calbert's row. "I'm glad we don't have any parts together. Do you think Ernie is as excited about the program as we are?" He asked Roland.

"No, I doubt he cares one bit. He probably thinks this is stupid," Roland answered. "I don't care anyway. I'm having fun."

"Roland, look, the background is up on the stage," he whispered. "It is awesome how they painted buildings and dirt streets to look so real. They also painted horses on the picture. Someone is a really good painter. There's a sheriff's office, a barbershop, and a restaurant for cowboys. This is so cool, Roland! I can't wait to sing my solo."

"They have even ladies painted in long dresses and cowboys," Roland added.

"The practice is starting. All the kids have to go up on stage and find their places to stand," he whispered to Roland.

"We practice singing the songs, and the kids with speaking parts practice talking between the songs," he whispered back to Calbert.

"It's almost time for my solo. It would be so awesome if there was someone in the audience tonight that would hear me sing, who could sign me up to be in a boys band. Never know, it could happen."

Chapter 15
Final Touches

Mrs. Baldwin announced to the students, "Everyone needs to be here at six- thirty tonight."

One kid raised his hand and said, "I don't know if I can remember the right time to tell my parents."

Mrs. Baldwin told them, "Don't worry, all of your parents received a letter about what time you need to be here tonight. They'll make sure you get here at the right time."

"I need a couple of students to go to the storage room and bring out a box of props for me," announced Mrs. Baldwin. Several hands went up into the air. "Thank you for all the volunteers, but I just need a couple of boys. Calbert and . . . let's see, Ernie. Will you two boys please go over to the storage room for me? The box is toward the back of the room and has prop pistols and shotguns for the show tonight in it. The side of the box is marked 'Western Props.'"

"I can't believe she picked Ernie out of all these kids in the program to go with me," Calbert whispered to Roland. "I feel sick, my mind is hazy, and I am having trouble thinking. He is going to beat me up."

"No, he won't, Calbert. Maybe if you try and talk to him nicely, he will be nice to you. Or just hurry up and run, so you don't have to spend time with him," Roland added with a smile. "You could probably outrun him."

"Very funny, Roland, you aren't the one that is about to get killed."

Calbert's legs were shaking when he tried to stand up. He kept hearing his mom's voice in his head saying, "When you are afraid, remember to pray because God is always with you." He also remembered her telling him to "pray for your enemies," and boy, was Ernie ever his enemy! He walked toward the storage room, he prayed, and a calm came over him that he was not expecting.

Ernie stood up and started walking toward Calbert like he was ready for a showdown. He was walking slowly and had that big mean smile on his face. He was looking right at Calbert with his eyes glaring brighter the closer he got to Calbert. Calbert could see that he had plans to kill him. Ernie wasn't much bigger than Calbert, but he was a lot tougher.

Chapter 16
The Fire

Ernie and Calbert walked into the storage room without saying a word to each other. Ernie dropped back so that Calbert would have to walk in first. Ernie came in and closed the door.

Calbert knew what that meant; he was going to get beat up. Calbert spun around and looked Ernie straight in the eye. *If he's going to hit me, he's going to have to look at me,* Calbert decided.

He tried to think of things to talk about. "So what is your favorite class?" Calbert asked nervously.

Ernie looked at him, and after a long pause, he said, "Art."

"What is it about art that you like?" Calbert asked, still a little nervous. He couldn't believe he was having a normal conversation with Ernie, but he wasn't very good at just talking.

Finally, Ernie said, "I'm pretty good in art. I like to draw and make things, and even my teacher likes me, I think." Ernie started to smile.

The room shook with the sound of an explosion. "Wow, did you feel that?"

"Yes, and I heard it too," Ernie replied. He was speaking faster than before. "What's happening?"

"I don't know!" Calbert answered.

"We better forget the box of props and get out of here," Ernie suggested. But when Ernie grabbed the doorknob, it came off in his hand.

"What are we going to do?" Calbert shouted. No answer came from Ernie.

"WHAT HAPPENED TO THE LIGHTS?" Ernie and Calbert both screamed at the same time.

"I can't see a thing. I think things are getting bad out there!"

Ernie shouted back, "Me too!"

"The lights keep flickering off and on. We have to get out of here and fast."

"My heart is beating so hard. I think my heart might pop out of my chest," Calbert added.

At that moment, a blasting, ear-piercing sound started ringing through the air. It felt like Calbert's ears were bleeding, and even covering them didn't seem to help. He looked at Ernie, and he was trying to plug his ears too. Calbert yelled, "What's that?" Ernie couldn't hear him over the loud ringing.

"Come on, we have to think now," Calbert yelled as he shook Ernie by the shoulders.

Ernie stuttered back, "The door locked, and we can't get out. And that's the fire alarm. I think the building is on fire. We can't open the door. We are stuck in this storage room with no way out!" Ernie yelled.

"Oh no, now what are we going to do?" asked Calbert

"The alarm is too loud. Nobody will be able to hear us yelling. I'm scared," yelled Ernie "What about you, Calbert?"

"Yes, I am really scared. Let's try to put the knob back. Maybe you can get it working.

Hurry, Ernie, and try it. I think I smell smoke!"

"The knob won't go back on," Ernie replied frantically. "There is no way to get the door open! I smell the smoke too!"

"I wonder if anyone has noticed we are missing yet!" yells Ernie, trying to be heard over the alarm. He paced back and forth. Then he said, "We have to think of something. Do you have any bright ideas on getting us out of here?"

"I don't know if anyone will notice. Maybe my friend Roland will tell someone we haven't come back yet," Calbert said trying to make both of them feel better.

"Let me try the door again. No, the knob just won't go back on, and the smell of smoke is getting stronger!"

Calbert shouted in a panic, "We are in trouble, Ernie! We have to think of something, or we are dead meat!"

"Can you hear all that screaming?" Ernie asked.

"Yes, it sounds like there are a lot of kids stuck in the building," he answered.

"Come on, Calbert, you're the smart one. Think!"

"You can think too, Ernie! You aren't stupid. Help me!"

Lisa Head

Chapter 17
Time for Action

Ernie looked around the room and said in a panic, "Let's look for rags and blankets in these boxes. We can use them to seal the cracks in the door. We have to keep the smoke out of here."

"Great idea! Let's do it. That will help us to breathe longer."

"We can also look for some kind of material to cover our faces. Remember to stay low to the floor."

"There has to be a way out!" Calbert shouted. "The door won't open, remember, Calbert!"

He looked up and saw a small window. "Look up there, Ernie. Do you think one of us could get out that way?"

"I *don't* know! Why are you asking me!" Ernie screamed back at Calbert. The lights kept going off and on while they listened to the sounds coming from outside the storage room.

"We can try to climb up to the window," Calbert suggested.

"Maybe if I put you on my shoulders, you can reach it," Ernie suggested.

"Okay, Ernie, let's try that."

"If I get you out, you better get me out of here fast!" Ernie said quickly.

"I will. I promise!" He tried to reassure Ernie. Calbert climbed on Ernie's shoulders, and he tried to stand.

"Whoa, I don't think I can stand up."

"You have to, if we are going to get out of here."

"Let's try stacking some boxes and see if that helps," Ernie suggested.

"There aren't enough. What's going to happen to us?"

"Nothing, just be quiet for a minute and let me think!" Ernie snapped back. Calbert felt his chest starting to burn. He couldn't stop coughing, and he could see Ernie holding his chest too. He was also coughing.

"Try one more time Calbert, get on my shoulders." Calbert climbed on and this time he reached the window.

"I got it! Give me a big push and I'll climb out and get help," Calbert yelled down to Ernie. With a big push from Ernie, Calbert got out the window.

Calbert ran as fast as he could. He found a fireman, and told him about Ernie being in the storage room.

Chapter 18
The Rescue

It became very quiet. There were no more screams and no more alarms, but the room was still filling with smoke.

Ernie stuffed more rags under the door. He couldn't stop coughing. *Wonder why it got so quiet all of a sudden. I have to sit down and catch my breath.*

"Is they're anybody in there?" A shout came from outside the storage room.

Ernie thought he heard something. *It sounds muffled, and there was a whoosh sound, but I'm sure it was a voice,* Ernie thought to himself.

Then he heard someone banging on the door, and again he heard, "Anyone in there?"

He was trying to yell, but his throat was too sore, and he could hardly make a sound.

Ernie saw a stick next to his leg. *I think I can reach the door from here.* He took the stick and started hitting the door as hard as he could with it.

The voice outside said, "Stay back from the door!" Ernie moved slowly in the other direction, but he had to scoot because he couldn't stand up any longer.

The door flew open with a loud crash and in walked the biggest toughest fireman Ernie had ever seen. He took off his oxygen mask and shared it with Ernie.

Another fireman came in and carried Ernie out of the school. They put him on a blanket next to the one Calbert was on.

A couple of other emergency medical technicians gave them their our own oxygen masks. The EMT's talked to them and asked them questions. Calbert mostly just nodded; his throat was better, but still hurt. Ernie was doing better too.

The medical people put Ernie and Calbert in the back of a big ambulance together. They turned on the siren, which was really awesome. "Ernie, are you feeling any better?"

"Yes, I'm feeling a lot better, how about you? Are you feeling better?"

"I'm a lot better, and I'm glad that is over with. I was scared."

Ernie laughed. "Me too! That was scary, but let's not tell anyone. Wouldn't be very cowboy like."

"I agree." Calbert smiled. "So you like cowboys too?" he asked Ernie.

"Yep, but I don't play much. No one at my house likes to play cowboys."

Nervously, he asked Ernie, "Would you like to come over to my house sometime and play cowboys with Roland and me?"

After a short silence, Ernie said, "Sure, that would be great. Thanks."

"Do you miss your dad a lot?" Calbert asked.

"Yes. Sometimes I like to remember all the fun we had together. I have brown hair and brown eyes like he did. People tell me I look a lot like my dad. I like it when people say that to me.

I think that is why Chuck doesn't like me. I remind him of my dad. I just try to stay out of his way, seems to work most of the time."

Ernie added. "He is okay but gets mad a lot, especially at me. So I spend most of my time being punished. Usually for something I didn't do anyway."

"I understand. I sometimes think about my birth family, and I miss them too. I am very happy to be with my forever family now, but I still think about the good times I had with my birth family. I might either smile or maybe cry when I start remembering.

I have forgotten a lot of stuff too, but I think I'll always remember the good stuff."

Chapter 19
New Beginnings

At the hospital, Ernie and Calbert were put in the same room to wait for their parents. "I have two brothers. How many brothers and sisters do you have?" He asked.

"Why do you ask so many questions?" Ernie asked, but his voice wasn't angry this time.

"I don't know. I get asked that a lot at home," Calbert said with a smile. The nurse brought in some clean clothes for them to put on; it was nice to get out of those stinky and dirty clothes they were wearing.

Ernie continued, "I have one sister, one stepbrother, and two stepsisters. My sister loves having sisters. They play together all the time." Ernie said with his eyes looking down at the floor.

"Do you like having a stepbrother?" Calbert asked.

"I would love to play with him, but he thinks I'm just a little kid, and he doesn't play with me much," Ernie answered sadly. "The only company I have is my best friend, Munch, the family dog. Munch is a mutt, but I can tell that he is very smart."

"Ever since my step dad and mom lost their jobs." Ernie continued, "things have been kind of rough. It was a lot better before they lost their jobs. I hope my parents find work soon. Sometimes I can hear them talking at night after I have gone to bed. I sneak partway down the stairs and listen to them."

"What happens?" Calbert asked. "My mother cries because she is worried. My step dad gets angry, but Mom just gets sad. I really liked things a lot better before. I wish things were the way they used to be."

Ernie suddenly stopped and said, "Hey, I'm sorry about all those mean things I have been doing to you. It's easy to get you rattled." And with a smile, he said, "I even think it's kind of cool that you are adopted."

"Thanks, I think it's kind of cool too!" Calbert grinned back at Ernie. He looked at Ernie and thought to himself, *He really isn't so bad after you get to know him.*

The nurse walked in with Calbert's mom, Ernie's mom, and Chuck. No one better get in his way as Calbert ran to his mom. She grabbed him and picked him up and was hugging way too hard, but that was okay—he liked it. Calbert thought she was even crying a little bit. She told him, "I was so worried about you, and I am so thankful you're all right!"

"What happened to the school?" Calbert asked.

"I think the electrical box exploded and set the school on fire. No program tonight, I'm afraid."

"That's okay. It 's been a long day anyway."

He looked over to Ernie. Ernie's mom and Chuck were hugging him. It looked to Calbert like Chuck liked Ernie. He could see they were all crying. He heard Chuck say, "I love you, Ernie. I'm so happy you are safe. I'm sorry I have been so hard on you. Let's try again. What do you think, Ernie? Want to give it a try?" He could see Ernie smiling.

Roland came into the hospital room. He was with Calbert's mom and Jason; he hadn't noticed they were there until just then.

"So what happened?" Roland asked.

"It was amazing—smoke everywhere! Ernie and I talked a lot, and he really isn't so bad. He likes cowboy stuff too. So what do you think, can he play with us sometime?" After some thought, Roland agrees.

Chapter 20
No Such Thing as Too Many Cowboys

"Mom, can Ernie come over after school sometime and play with Roland and me?" Calbert asked.

"Sure, I don't see why not. I'll give his mom a call and let her know Ernie is welcome to come over to play."

Then Jason piped up, "Thought you didn't like that kid!"

"Oh, be quiet, Jason! He's okay. Plus he likes cowboys, so he's pretty awesome."

Sticking up for Calbert, Roland agreed.

"Look, there's Papa's truck!" Calbert jumped out of the car and ran into the house.

"It's about time you got here," he teases me. "Are you okay? Do you feel better?"

"I'm fine, Papa."

"I am so sorry about your music program getting cancelled. You will get a chance to sing again soon."

"I hope so," he replied.

"Ethan, get off my lap, and let's go play."

"No, I want to play with Papa!"

"Then go play with him and get off my lap."

"Come on, Roland, let's go to the tree house."

Roland and Calbert raced out the door, jumped on our bikes and pedal as fast as they could for the tree house.

"Thanks, for pulling up the ladder, Roland, I just wanted to get away from everyone for a while. A lot happened today, and I want to talk to my best friend. I was scared in the fire. We were locked in the storage room and couldn't get the door to open."

"Look, bad guys!" Roland shouted, trying to change the subject. Calbert grabbed his pistols and started shooting.

While Roland covered him, he popped up and started shooting. Then suddenly, he saw another red bike. He stopped shooting and realized it is Ernie. He had come over to play.

"Ernie is here. Let down the ladder." He climbed down the ladder to greet Ernie.

"Hey, Ernie, I'm glad you are here."

"Thanks, I brought my six-shooters, shotgun, and my favorite cowboy hat."

"YAY! Come on up. There are a lot of bad guys out there in the cornfields. Roland and I need your help."

Up the ladder, Ernie and Calbert went. Roland greeted them with guns and waved to them which direction to go. They all ducked down, and in the cowboy way, they started shooting the bad guys.

"Those guys don't have a chance with the three of us protecting this tree house."

"Three toughest cowboys in the state!" They all smiled in agreement.

"Like I always say, three cowboys are better than two."

"Over there, look! Twenty, maybe thirty, marauders heading right for the tree house," Calbert whispered to Roland and Ernie. They took cover behind the wall of the tree house to get their pistols and shotguns ready.

"Bang bang bang, there go six." Calbert ducks down while bullets whiz over their heads.

"Kapow kapow!" shouts Roland. "Just got four of them!" Like a shot, Calbert pops back up and started shooting, while Roland was reloading.

"Bang bang bang, down goes five more."

Up jumped Ernie. *Pow, pow, zing, zang, pow.* Ernie blew into the end of his pistols and put them back in his holster. "No more bad guys. We finished them all off. We are just too tough for that bunch of outlaws!"

They all laughed and cheered.

THE END

ABOUT THE AUTHOR

Lisa Head is an elementary music teacher and foster/adoptive parent. She has fostered children for several years. She has taught music for over 26 years in a nearby public school system. Lisa has cared for and worked with many traditional and therapeutic children throughout the years. She lives in Plymouth Indiana, with her three sons, two dogs, cat and bunny.

Calbert: The Third-Grade Cowboy

.

CPSIA information can be obtained at www.ICGtesting.com
Printed in the USA
LVOW132143170612

286537LV00007B/15/P